D1591666

Hockey
LEGENDS

Blaine Wiseman

Go to **www.av2books.com**, and enter this book's unique code.

BOOK CODE

H768362

AV² by Weigl brings you media enhanced books that support active learning.

AV² provides enriched content that supplements and complements this book. Weigl's AV² books strive to create inspired learning and engage young minds in a total learning experience.

Your AV² Media Enhanced books come alive with...

Audio
Listen to sections of the book read aloud.

Key Words
Study vocabulary, and complete a matching word activity.

Video
Watch informative video clips.

Quizzes
Test your knowledge.

Embedded Weblinks
Gain additional information for research.

Slide Show
View images and captions, and prepare a presentation.

Try This!
Complete activities and hands-on experiments.

... and much, much more!

Published by AV² by Weigl
350 5th Avenue, 59th Floor
New York, NY 10118
Website: www.av2books.com

Library of Congress Control Number: 2016956748

ISBN 978-1-4896-4803-7 (hardcover)
ISBN 978-1-4896-5051-1 (softcover)
ISBN 978-1-4896-4804-4 (multi-user eBook)

Printed in the United States of America, in Brainerd, Minnesota
1 2 3 4 5 6 7 8 9 21 20 19 18 17

072017
310117

Project Coordinator: Jared Siemens
Designer: Terry Paulhus

Photo Credits
Every reasonable effort has been made to trace ownership and to obtain permission to reprint copyright material. The publisher would be pleased to have any errors or omissions brought to their attention so that they may be corrected in subsequent printings. The publisher acknowledges Getty Images, iStock, and Alamy as its primary image suppliers for this title.

Hockey
LEGENDS

Contents

History and Culture

I ce hockey has a very long history. Games similar to modern ice hockey were played in **ancient** Egypt, Persia, and China. The first recorded game of hockey on ice was played in 1850. In the early days, ice hockey was only played outdoors. The puck was made from a lacrosse ball cut in half, or a circular piece of wood. On March 3, 1875, James Creighton of Montreal, Canada, staged the first indoor public hockey game. This got people interested in the sport. Teams and leagues soon began forming all over Canada and the United States.

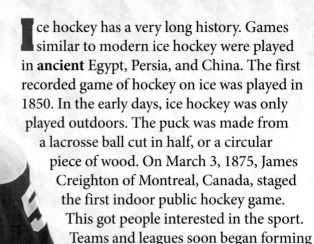

Professional hockey players come from all over the world. Swedish player Nicklas Lidström played for the Detroit Red Wings for 20 seasons.

The Boston Bruins were the first NHL team in the United States. The team formed in 1924.

Hockey Slang

Part of hockey culture involves its unique language, or slang. For example, hockey players refer to an ice rink as a "barn." A very exciting game is called a "barn burner." Pucks are nicknamed "biscuits." A player who "rides the pine" is a player who sits on the bench for the entire game. If a game has a lot of fights or penalties, it is called a "gongshow." This slang is always growing and changing.

Fan Tradition

Hockey fans occasionally throw items onto the rink to show their enthusiasm, or their frustration. In Toronto, a fan who wanted to "wake up the team" tossed a toaster waffle onto the ice. Fans of Andrew Hammond, of the Ottawa Senators, have been known to throw hamburgers onto the ice because of his nickname "The Hamburglar." Detroit Red Wings fans throw octopuses onto the ice. This tradition dates back to 1952, when two fans who owned a seafood shop threw an octopus onto the ice. The eight legs of the octopus represented the eight wins needed to win the championship.

Fighting in Hockey

Collisions, both intentional and unintentional, are common in hockey. These collisions sometimes lead to fights. In the 1970s, fighting during games grew more common. Teams would hire "enforcers" to intimidate other players. Some brawls involved entire teams. Over the past several years, the number of fights during games has gone down. In the NHL, players who fight receive a five-minute penalty, and they have to leave the game for five minutes. In international leagues, fighting players are ejected from the game.

The Stanley Cup

The Pittsburgh Penguins won the 2017 Stanley Cup, defeating the Nashville Predators 4–2 in a six-game series.

The National Hockey League (NHL) was formed in 1917. It quickly became the leading **league** in the world. It consists of 23 teams in the United States and 7 teams in Canada. At the end of each season, the winner of the NHL playoff game receives the Stanley Cup.

The Stanley Cup was first presented in 1893. Lord Frederick Arthur Stanley, a devoted fan, donated the Cup in 1889. At that time, it was the trophy for the Canadian Amateur Hockey Association. The first team to win the Stanley Cup was the Montreal Amateur Athletic Association. In 1926, the Stanley Cup became the championship trophy of the NHL. Today, there are seven games in the NHL championship series.

The Stanley Cup has grown taller over the years as more names have been added to it. Today, it stands almost 35.25 inches (89.54 centimeters) tall and weighs 34.5 pounds (15.6 kilograms).

STANLEY CUP RECORDS

19 GOALS — Over his 24-year career, Chris Chelios scored the **most goals** in one playoff year.

23 SHUTOUTS — Patrick Roy played for 19 years and holds the record for career **playoff shutouts**.

82 PLAYOFFS — The Montreal Canadiens have been in the **playoffs** more times than any other team.

122 GOALS — Over his 20-year career, Wayne Gretzky scored the **highest number of playoff goals**.

266 GAMES — Chris Chelios has played in **more playoff games** than any other player.

24 Hours with the Cup

When a team wins the Stanley Cup, the name of every player, coach, and front-office employee is **engraved** onto it. The team keeps the cup for one year, and everyone gets 24 hours to spend with it. People get to choose what to do with the cup, as long as it is kept safe. Willie Mitchell of the Los Angeles Kings took the Stanley Cup on his boat while fishing. Sylvain Lefebvre of the Colorado Avalanche used it as his daughter's **baptismal font**.

STANLEY CUP WINNERS

- Montreal Canadiens — **23**
- Toronto Maple Leafs — **13**
- Detroit Red Wings — **11**
- Boston Bruins — **6**
- Chicago Blackhawks — **6**

Hockey Equipment

Hockey is a physical sport, with players moving at fast speeds on sharp skates. Protective equipment is essential to keep athletes safe. The first hockey games were played outdoors on natural ice, so the first equipment was intended to keep players warm. In 1880, players used leather strips to protect their shins. The first gloves were made of leather, animal fur, and felt. As technology has advanced, players' equipment has evolved to focus on safety and speed.

UNIFORM

Hockey uniforms today are constructed of several different types of pads. These pads cover a player's shoulders, elbows, wrists, knees, and shins. The pads are made of hard plastic. Some, like the elbow pads, have foam on the outside to protect other players. These pads keep all players safe, while still allowing players to move easily and quickly.

Professional hockey teams wear home uniforms at their own arena, and away uniforms at other teams' arenas. Since 2004, NHL teams wear colored jerseys at home and white jerseys while away.

The Nashville Predators wear white jerseys with yellow and black accents when away, and yellow jerseys while playing at home.

HOCKEY STICK

Hockey sticks were originally made from ash, birch, or willow wood. Some hockey sticks are still made from wood today, but most are made from a combination of fiberglass, aluminum, carbon fiber, titanium, or **Kevlar**®. These "composite" sticks are lighter and more durable than wood. Hockey sticks measure between 46 and 63 inches (116.8 and 134.6 cm) in length. A player's hockey-stick length is determined by their height, position, and skating style.

HOCKEY SKATES

In the 1500s, skates were made of narrow strips of metal connected to a block of wood. The wood block had straps that fastened to the bottom of a player's boot. By 1914, design changes such as double blades and a toe pick had been added. Today, ice hockey skates today have no toe pick. They fit lower on the ankle and have thicker blades than early designs.

HOCKEY PUCK

Modern hockey pucks are made from rubber. They are three inches wide and one inch thick. Because hockey pucks are flat, they usually slide along the ice rather than bouncing, like a regular ball would. Pucks are frozen to reduce bouncing even further. Frozen pucks are so important that officials will replace a used one with a frozen puck every two minutes during a game.

HELMET

In the early days of hockey, players did not wear helmets. That changed in 1968, when Minnesota player Bill Masterson died after hitting his head on the ice. By 1979, the NHL made wearing a helmet mandatory. Today, helmets are made of high-tech plastic. Goaltenders' helmets have specialized face masks.

Greatest Legends

Most NHL players started playing hockey when they were very young. Almost all of them played on college teams or in the "Major Juniors," which are lower-level professional leagues. In addition to superior ice-skating skills, professional hockey athletes must be physically tough. Only five percent of these athletes end up playing in the NHL. Below are two ice hockey legends.

Wayne Gretzky

Nicknamed "The Great One," Wayne Gretzky is considered hockey's most-celebrated player. He holds or shares 61 records. Gretzky was born in Brantford, Ontario, and started playing hockey when he was only 2 years old. In 1984, Gretzky won his first Stanley Cup with the Edmonton Oilers. During his 20-year career he also played for the Los Angeles Kings, St. Louis Blues, and New York Rangers. He retired in 1999, but later became a coach and manager. He was also the director of the Canadian men's Olympic hockey team, and he led the 2002 team to a gold medal. Gretzky was a part-owner of the NHL Phoenix Coyotes from 2001 to 2009, and served as their head coach from 2005 to 2009.

Manon Rhéaume

Manon Rhéaume was born in Lac Beauport, Quebec. She was the first and only woman to play in an NHL hockey game. In 1992, she played as goalie for the Tampa Bay Lightning against the St. Louis Blues. She was 20 years old. Rhéaume faced nine shots and stopped seven of them. In the 1998 Olympics, she played for the Canadian women's team and won a silver medal.

Most Goals in One Season

Wayne Gretzky set the record for the most goals in one hockey season, during the 1981–82 season. That record still holds 34 years later. The records below show the top five scorers in a single season.

Wayne Gretzky, 92 (1981–82)

Phil Esposito, 76 (1970–71)

Brett Hull, 86 (1990–91)

Mario Lemieux, 85 (1988–89)

Teemu Selänne , 76 (1992–93)

Career Shutouts

A goaltender's job is to prevent the other team from scoring. If the goaltender **blocks** all of the opposing team's goals during a game, it is called a shutout. These five goaltenders hold the record for the most shutouts.

PLAYER	SHUTOUTS
Martin Brodeur	125
Terry Sawchuk	103
George Hainsworth	94
Glenn Hall	84
Jacques Plante	82

Willie O'Ree

In 1958, Willie O'Ree became the first African American athlete to play in the NHL. He first played for the Boston Bruins during a game against the Montreal Canadiens. He played intermittently for the Bruins until 1961 and was known for being a fast skater. O'Ree was blind in one eye, which he kept a secret during his entire professional hockey career.

Fastest Skater

The NHL holds an All-Star SuperSkills Competition every year. Players are timed as they skate around a designated course. In 2016, these were the fastest skaters.

PLAYER	SECONDS
Dylan Larkin	12.894
Roman Josi	13.527
Brandon Saad	13.634
Taylor Hall	13.654
Matt Duchene	14.026

At the SuperSkills Competition in 2016, Dylan Larkin broke the record for the fastest skater. The previous record was set in 1996 by Mike Gartner of the Toronto Maple Leafs.

Scoring and Assisting

Ryane Clowe played for the San Jose Sharks from 2005 to 2012, and was a top scorer. He earned a career-high 34 points during the 2006–07 season.

To score a goal in hockey, the puck must cross the goal line between two goal posts and pass under the goal crossbar. When a goal is made after a series of passes, it is called an assist. Two assists can be awarded on one scoring play. The player who passes to the scorer is awarded an assist. This is called a primary assist. Additionally, the teammate who got the puck to the passer will also receive an assist. This is a secondary assist.

Individual players receive **points** for both goals and assists. These points are different than the playoff points a team receives based on a game's outcome. Individual points go toward a player's career statistics. Team points determine that team's spot in the playoffs.

In 2014, Matt Calvert scored a game-winning goal that earned the Columbus Blue Jackets their first Stanley Cup Playoff win.

Career Goals

A hockey goal is worth one point. Career goals are the total number of goals an individual player has scored during his or her professional career. These five players have scored the highest number of career goals.

PLAYER	GOALS
Wayne Gretzky	894
Gordie Howe	801
Jaromír Jágr	749
Brett Hull	741
Marcel Dionne	731

Career Assists

Most NHL athletes play for an average of 3.5 years. The athletes with the most assists have played for an average of 21.8 years. These five players hold the records for most career assists.

PLAYER	ASSISTS
Wayne Gretzky	1,963
Ron Francis	1,731
Mark Messier	1,193
Ray Bourque	1,169
Paul Coffey	1,135

Career Points

A player's career points are a combination of his or her number of goals and assists. This combined number can be higher than their career goals. The five players below have the most career points.

PLAYER	POINTS
Wayne Gretzky	2,857
Mark Messier	1,887
Jaromír Jágr	1,868
Gordie Howe	1,850
Ron Francis	1,798

Most Team Points in a Season

A team receives two points for a win and one point for a tie. If a game goes into overtime, both teams receive a point. The Montreal Canadiens and the Detroit Redwings hold the top five spots for most team points in a season.

132	Montreal Canadiens (1976–1977)
129	Montreal Canadiens (1977–1978)
127	Montreal Canadiens (1975–1976)
124	Detroit Red Wings (1995–1996)
121	Detroit Red Wings (2005–2006)

Mark Messier was a strong leader and a top scorer. His teams won six Stanley Cups, and he was named the league's Most Valuable Player twice.

Money Makers

Professional hockey is a big business. NHL teams are highly valuable. A professional hockey player can earn a large salary. This depends on their level of skill and how excited fans are to see them play. For fans, the cost of attending a game depends on the team's popularity. Currently, Toronto Maple Leaf tickets are the most expensive. Most are more than US$100. The average hockey fan will spend a little more than $100 at each game.

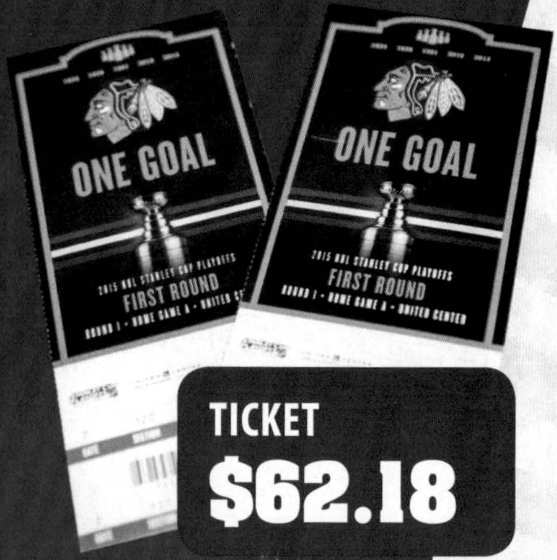

TICKET
$62.18

HOT DOG
$4.94

PARKING
$17.70

CAP
$19.75

TOTAL
$104.57

Business of Hockey

A mix of individuals and corporations own the most valuable teams in the NHL. The New York Rangers are owned by The Madison Square Garden Company, which also owns the team's home arena. The top five most valuable teams are listed below.

$1.25 BILLION	New York Rangers
$1.12 BILLION	Montreal Canadiens
$1.1 BILLION	Toronto Maple Leafs
$925 MILLION	Chicago Blackhawks
$800 MILLION	Boston Bruins

Signing Bonus

In addition to annual salaries, many hockey players receive signing bonuses for joining or staying with a team. These bonuses can make up most of their income. In 2015, Nashville Predators defenseman Shea Weber received a $13 million signing bonus in addition to his $1 million salary.

Sporting Salaries

A professional hockey player can earn millions of dollars. That money comes from a combination of sponsorships, signing bonus, and salary. These athletes are paid the most money for their sport annually.

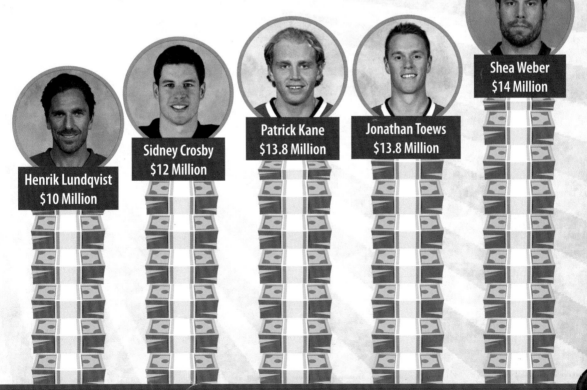

Henrik Lundqvist
$10 Million

Sidney Crosby
$12 Million

Patrick Kane
$13.8 Million

Jonathan Toews
$13.8 Million

Shea Weber
$14 Million

Hockey Stadiums of North America

Inside a hockey stadium is an ice rink. It is rectangular in shape, and has rounded corners. Surrounding the ice is a wall called the boards. Though every professional hockey rink is the same standard size, different venues offer different challenges. Lighting patterns, size and color of the boards, and seating capacity all impact the feel of a stadium. This map shows four of the most renowned hockey rinks in the United States and Canada.

Alberta

Saskatchewan

CANA

British Columbia

Washington

Oregon

Nevada

Utah

Colorado

California

New Mexico

Arizona

UNITE
STAT
MEXICO

BELL CENTRE
Montreal, Quebec, Canada

Bell Centre has the largest capacity of any hockey arena in the NHL. It holds 21,273 people.

VERIZON CENTER
Washington, D.C., United States

Home of the Washington Capitals, the Verizon Center is the largest hockey arena by size. The interior is about 1,000,000 square feet (92,903 square meters).

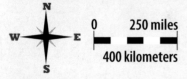

N
W E
S

0   250 miles

400 kilometers

Pacific Ocean

LEGEND

■ United States   ■ Canada

□ Water   ■ Other Countries

BARCLAYS CENTER
New York City, New York, United States

Completed in 2012, the Barclays Center was the most expensive arena to build. It cost $1.03 billion.

MATTHEWS ARENA
Boston, Massachusetts, United States

The Boston Bruins' Matthews Arena was first opened in 1910. It is the world's oldest hockey arena that is still in use.

Coaches and Referees

In addition to training players, hockey coaches determine the **strategy** of a game. They have to make quick decisions based on how a game is progressing. NHL teams have one head coach and several assistant coaches. They also have a goaltending coach who works with the team's goalie.

Scotty Bowman

Scotty Bowman coached for 30 seasons in the NHL and is considered the greatest hockey coach of all time. Bowman won more than 65 percent of his NHL games. This is more than any other coach in history. Bowman also holds the record for most losses in NHL history.

Scotty Bowman by the Numbers

2,141	Most Regular-Season Games Coached
1,244	Most Regular-Season Wins
353	Most Playoff Games Coached
223	Most Playoff Wins
9	Most Stanley Cups Won by a Coach

In the 1970s, Scotty Bowman coached the Montreal Canadiens. He won four consecutive Stanley Cups while with the team.

Joel Quenneville coached the Chicago Blackhawks to a Stanley Cup victory in 2015.

Ray Scapinello

Linesmen are officials responsible for certain fouls called infractions. They also break up fights. Ray "Scampy" Scapinello is considered the Wayne Gretzky of linesmen. In his 33-year NHL career, he did not miss a single game. He was also selected to be an official at the 1998 Olympics in Nagano, Japan.

The Winningest Coaches

Effective coaches have to be strong leaders. They must also have excellent technical knowledge about hockey. Coaches need to have passion for the game, and a deep commitment to helping each player succeed. These coaches lead the NHL for total number of victories.

COACH	WINS
Scotty Bowman	1,244
Joel Quenneville	783
Al Arbour	782

The Referees

Referees have to be very skilled skaters. They must be able to officiate without interfering with the game. These referees have officiated the most games in NHL history.

OFFICIAL	OFFICIATED
Kerry Fraser	1,904
Bill McCreary	1,737
Don Koharski	1,719

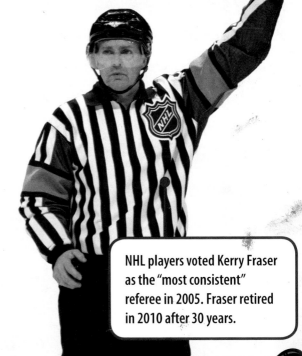

NHL players voted Kerry Fraser as the "most consistent" referee in 2005. Fraser retired in 2010 after 30 years.

Most Valuable Players

Each year, a panel of NHL writers and journalists award one hockey player the Hart Memorial Trophy and name him the Most Valuable Player. The Hart Memorial Trophy winner is the player that has been the biggest value to his team. Other things that are considered are the number of games played during the season, and whether the player has already been an MVP in the past. These six players are the top Hart Memorial Trophy winners.

Wayne Gretzky

1980–1987, 1989 MVP • CENTER • LOS ANGELES KINGS

Gretzky won his first Hart Memorial Trophy while playing for the Edmonton Oilers in 1980. It was the first time a first-year player received the award. He went on to win the trophy nine times, the most of any NHL player in history. Gretzky currently holds the records for most goals made in regular season, at 894. He was inducted into the Hockey Hall of Fame in 1999.

Gordie Howe

1952, 1953 ,1957, 1958, 1960, 1963 MVP • RIGHT WING • DETROIT RED WINGS

Known as "Mr. Hockey," Gordie Howe received the Hart Memorial Trophy six times. Howe started with the Detroit Red Wings in the late 1940s, winning his first MVP award in 1952. That first MVP-winning year, Howe scored 47 goals. In 1953, he beat his own career record by scoring a career high of 49 goals. He played his last game in 1997, making him the only NHL player whose career spanned six decades.

Eddie Shore

1933, 1935, 1936, 1938 MVP • DEFENSE • BOSTON BRUINS

Eddie Shore is considered one of the greatest defensemen of all time. Nicknamed "Old Blood and Guts," he was known for being aggressive during games. During the 1927–28 season, he set the single-season record for penalty minutes, with 165 minutes. He received the Hart Memorial Trophy four times in the 1930s for his efforts with the Bruins.

Alexander Ovechkin

2008, 2009, 2013 MVP • LEFT WING • WASHINGTON CAPITALS

Alexander Ovechkin was born in Moscow, Russia, and received the Hart Memorial Trophy in 2008, 2009, and 2013. By the time he was 17, Ovechkin was already considered a top player. The Washington Capitals **drafted** him in 2004. During the 2007–08 season, Ovechkin scored a career-high 65 goals. The next season, he attempted a career-high 528 shots on goal. Ovechkin scored 25 power play goals during the 2012–13 season, a career high. He has also been a member of two Russian Olympic teams.

Bobby Orr

1970, 1971, 1972 MVP • DEFENSE • BOSTON BRUINS

The Boston Bruins scouted Bobby Orr when he was a teenager, and arranged for him to train with a junior league. At age 18, Orr started his NHL career. He won the Hart Memorial Trophy in 1970 for the game-winning goal that secured the Bruins a Stanley Cup victory. He went on to win the Hart Memorial Trophy two more times, in 1971 and 1972.

Howie Morenz

1928, 1931, 1932 MVP • CENTER • MONTREAL CANADIENS

In the 1920s and 1930s, Howie Morenz was considered the greatest hockey player in the world. Morenz played for the Montreal Canadiens, and received three Hart Memorial Trophies for his efforts with the team. He also won multiple Stanley Cups. In 1932, Morenz played a career-high 48 games. In 1937, he broke his leg during a game, and he later died from complications.

Quiz

Now that you have read about hockey legends, test your knowledge by answering these questions. All of the information can be found in the text. The answers are also provided for reference.

1 What is Wayne Gretzky's nickname?

A: The Great One

2 What is the NHL championship trophy called?

A: The Stanley Cup

3 What do Detroit Red Wings fans occasionally throw onto the ice?

A: Octopuses

4 Which NHL arena was the most expensive to build?

A: Barclays Center

5 What are modern pucks made from?

A: Rubber

6 Who was the first African American to play in the NHL?

A: Willie O'Ree

7 What does it mean when a player "rides the pine"?

A: It means he or she sits on the bench for the entire game.

8 Which team has won the most Stanley Cups?

A: The Montreal Canadiens

Key Words

ancient: belonging to the very distant past and no longer in existence

baptismal font: the place holy water is kept for a religious blessing

blocks: prevents from entering

drafted: chosen to play for a team

engraved: carved words and numbers into an object

inducted: chosen to be a member

Kevlar®: an engineered fiber commonly used in helmets and vests

league: a group of people who come together for a common purpose

linesmen: hockey officials who work with referees

points: the sum of the number of goals and assists a player scores

strategy: a plan of action

Index

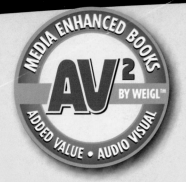

Log on to www.av2books.com

AV² by Weigl brings you media enhanced books that support active learning. Go to www.av2books.com, and enter the special code found on page 2 of this book. You will gain access to enriched and enhanced content that supplements and complements this book. Content includes video, audio, weblinks, quizzes, a slide show, and activities.

AV² Online Navigation

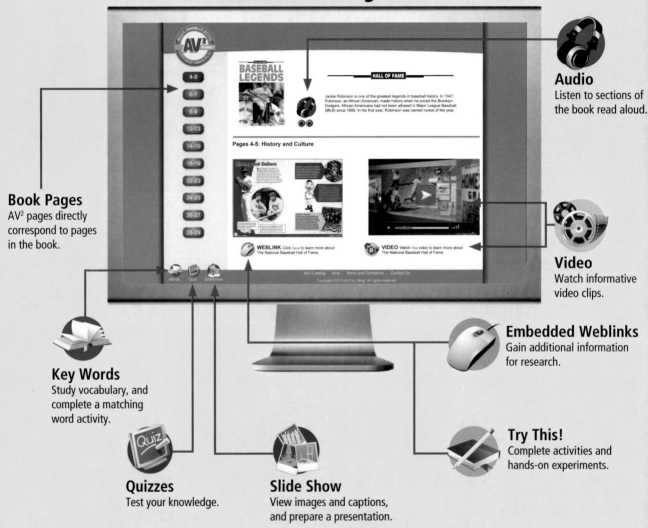

Audio
Listen to sections of the book read aloud.

Book Pages
AV² pages directly correspond to pages in the book.

Video
Watch informative video clips.

Key Words
Study vocabulary, and complete a matching word activity.

Embedded Weblinks
Gain additional information for research.

Quizzes
Test your knowledge.

Slide Show
View images and captions, and prepare a presentation.

Try This!
Complete activities and hands-on experiments.

AV² was built to bridge the gap between print and digital. We encourage you to tell us what you like and what you want to see in the future.

Sign up to be an AV² Ambassador at www.av2books.com/ambassador.